COUNT-A-SAURUS

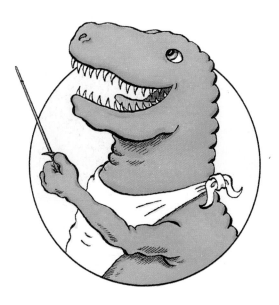

by Nancy Blumenthal

illustrated by Robert Jay Kaufman

Four Winds Press   New York

for
Jake and Ben
and for
Rebecca and Sara

Grateful acknowledgment to David D. Gillette, Ph.D., state paleontologist of Utah, for his expert reading of this manuscript. And special thanks to Cindy Kane, our editor, and Cecilia Yung, our art director.

The text of this book is set in 18 point Palatino.
The illustrations are rendered in pen-and-ink and watercolor.

LIBRARY OF CONGRESS CATALOGING-IN-PUBLICATION DATA Blumenthal, Nancy. Count-a-saurus/ by Nancy Blumenthal; illustrated by Robert Jay Kaufman.—1st American ed.   p.   cm. Summary: Depicts numbered groups of dinosaurs and other prehistoric creatures, from one Stegosaurus standing in the sun to ten Hadrosaurids sporting funny hats. Additional text in the back provides more information about each species.   ISBN 0-02-749391-1   1. Counting—Juvenile literature. 2. Dinosaurs—Juvenile literature. [1. Dinosaurs. 2. Counting.] I. Kaufman, Robert Jay, ill. II. Title. QA113.B57 1989   513'.2—dc19   [E]   88-21320 CIP AC

1 One Stegosaurus standing in the sun.
(Steg-o-SOAR-us)

Two Compsognathus always on the run.
(Comp-so-GNAY-thus)

Three Allosaurus gnashing pointy teeth.
(Al-o-SOAR-us)

Four Iguanodon scratching itchy feet.
(Ig-WAN-o-don)

5 Five Archaeopteryx gliding to a rock.
(Ar-kee-OP-tur-iks)

Six Ceratopsians wearing frills and purple socks.
(Ser-a-TOP-see-ans)

7

Seven Plesiosaurus swimming in the seas.
(Plee-zee-o-SOAR-us)

Eight Brontosaurus browsing in the trees.
(Bron-toe-SOAR-us)

9 Nine Ankylosaurus with armor on their backs.
(Ann-kie-lo-SOAR-us)

Ten Hadrosaurids sporting funny hats.
(Had-ro-SOAR-ids)

Now one to ten we sing the chorus....

This is how we count-a-saurus!

One Stegosaurus standing in the sun.

Why did Stegosaurus have those bony plates on its back? The sharp, angular plates might have helped Stegosaurus protect itself. Scientists also think the plates may have served as an early solar heating-cooling system for Stegosaurus. Those bony plates were full of tiny blood vessels. Standing sideways to the sun could have been Stegosaurus's method of warming up! When Stegosaurus got too warm it could change position and face directly into the sun. Then the rays would pass over the bony plates and this plant-eating dinosaur could cool off.

Two Compsognathus always on the run.

Compsognathus was one of the smallest dinosaurs. No bigger than a chicken, it had long, thin legs and was a speedy runner. A light frame enabled this carnivore, or meat-eater, to catch other fast-moving animals such as small lizards or dragonflies.

Three Allosaurus gnashing pointy teeth.

Allosaurus was another carnivorous dinosaur. Many of us think of the meat-eating dinosaurs as mean and ferocious. But it's important to remember they were just following their instincts. They attacked their prey in order to survive and only when they were hungry.

Four Iguanodon scratching itchy feet.

Did you notice the spiked thumbs on Iguanodon's forearms? For years people thought those spikes belonged on the end of Iguanodon's nose, making it look like a rhinoceros. Then scientists found whole Iguanodon skeletons and saw the spikes attached to the Iguanodon's hands.

Five Archaeopteryx gliding to a rock.

What a sight it would have been to see this primitive creature swoop down from the sky and land on a tree or rock. Because Archaeopteryx had feathers it is considered a bird, not a dinosaur. However, it did not have the necessary bone structure to flap its wings, so it could not fly. Still, with a good running start into the wind, it could certainly have become airborne.

Monoclonius
(Mah-no-CLO-nee-us)

Styracosaurus
(Sty-rack-o-SOAR-us)

Triceratops
(Tri-SAIR-o-tops)

Six Ceratopsians wearing frills and purple socks.

Ceratopsian is the group name for the horned dinosaurs. The number of horns varied, as did the size and shape of the frill around the Ceratopsian's head. Scientists speculate that the frill helped to guard the dinosaur's neck as well as to provide some muscular support for the animal's large head. Scissorlike teeth helped these herbivores, or plant-eaters, chomp on tough leaves and fronds. They grazed in herds, much like cattle would graze in a field today.

Seven Plesiosaurus swimming in the seas.

Plesiosaurus was a marine reptile that lived when dinosaurs did. Using its limbs as paddles, Plesiosaurus moved about freely in the water, probably dining on fish and other marine life. It is not known whether Plesiosaurus gave birth to live young, the way dolphins and whales do, or if it laid reptilian eggs on land.

Eight Brontosaurus browsing in the trees.

You could probably recognize this all-time favorite dinosaur in your sleep! Brontosaurus is the popular name for the dinosaur scientists call Apatosaurus (Uh-pat-o-SOAR-us). This huge plant-eater probably traveled in herds. Paleontologists, scientists who study fossils, think the larger adults may have walked on the outside of the herd in order to protect their young from meat-eating dinosaurs.

Nine Ankylosaurus with armor on their backs.

This dinosaur had some of the best protection around. It had a hard, bony back like a turtle's, but it probably couldn't tuck its legs and head under its armor plating, the way a turtle can. Bony plates, spikes, and a heavy club tail made Ankylosaurus a tough opponent.

Corythosaurus
(Cor-ith-o-SOAR-us)

Lambeosaurus
(Lam-bee-o-SOAR-us)

Parasaurolophus
(Pair-a-soar-AWL-o-fuss)

Ten Hadrosaurids sporting funny hats.

"Duckbills" is the common, everyday name given to this wonderful-looking group of creatures. Even though their broad snouts looked "ducklike," Hadrosaurids lived on land, browsing on such vegetation as twigs, pine needles, and fruit. Many of these dinosaurs had crests on top of their heads. Different-shaped crests may have helped the various kinds of duckbills recognize each other during the mating season. Crests may also have aided the duckbills in calling to each other; the sound might have been amplified as it passed through the hollow tubes and spaces inside.

Five Archaeopteryx gliding to a rock.

What a sight it would have been to see this primitive creature swoop down from the sky and land on a tree or rock. Because Archaeopteryx had feathers it is considered a bird, not a dinosaur. However, it did not have the necessary bone structure to flap its wings, so it could not fly. Still, with a good running start into the wind, it could certainly have become airborne.

Monoclonius
(Mah-no-CLO-nee-us)

Styracosaurus
(Sty-rack-o-SOAR-us)

Triceratops
(Tri-SAIR-o-tops)

Six Ceratopsians wearing frills and purple socks.

Ceratopsian is the group name for the horned dinosaurs. The number of horns varied, as did the size and shape of the frill around the Ceratopsian's head. Scientists speculate that the frill helped to guard the dinosaur's neck as well as to provide some muscular support for the animal's large head. Scissorlike teeth helped these herbivores, or plant-eaters, chomp on tough leaves and fronds. They grazed in herds, much like cattle would graze in a field today.

Seven Plesiosaurus swimming in the seas.

Plesiosaurus was a marine reptile that lived when dinosaurs did. Using its limbs as paddles, Plesiosaurus moved about freely in the water, probably dining on fish and other marine life. It is not known whether Plesiosaurus gave birth to live young, the way dolphins and whales do, or if it laid reptilian eggs on land.

Eight Brontosaurus browsing in the trees.

You could probably recognize this all-time favorite dinosaur in your sleep! Brontosaurus is the popular name for the dinosaur scientists call Apatosaurus (Uh-pat-o-SOAR-us). This huge plant-eater probably traveled in herds. Paleontologists, scientists who study fossils, think the larger adults may have walked on the outside of the herd in order to protect their young from meat-eating dinosaurs.

Nine Ankylosaurus with armor on their backs.

This dinosaur had some of the best protection around. It had a hard, bony back like a turtle's, but it probably couldn't tuck its legs and head under its armor plating, the way a turtle can. Bony plates, spikes, and a heavy club tail made Ankylosaurus a tough opponent.

Corythosaurus
(Cor-ith-o-SOAR-us)

Lambeosaurus
(Lam-bee-o-SOAR-us)

Parasaurolophus
(Pair-a-soar-AWL-o-fuss)

Ten Hadrosaurids sporting funny hats.

"Duckbills" is the common, everyday name given to this wonderful-looking group of creatures. Even though their broad snouts looked "ducklike," Hadrosaurids lived on land, browsing on such vegetation as twigs, pine needles, and fruit. Many of these dinosaurs had crests on top of their heads. Different-shaped crests may have helped the various kinds of duckbills recognize each other during the mating season. Crests may also have aided the duckbills in calling to each other; the sound might have been amplified as it passed through the hollow tubes and spaces inside.